LAMB CHOP'S PLAY-ALONG FAIRY TALE

CINDERELLA

retold by **Shari Lewis**

illustrated by Jane Caminos

A LITTLE ROOSTER BOOK

NEW YORK · TORONTO · LONDON · SYDNEY · AUCKLAND

CINDERELLA
Lamb Chop's Play-Along Fairy Tale

A Little Rooster Book/July, 1994

Little Rooster is a trademark of Bantam Doubleday Dell Books for
Young Readers, a division of Bantam Doubleday Dell Publishing Group, Inc.

ISBN 0-553-37386-2

Printed simultaneously in the United States and Canada

Little Rooster Books are published by Bantam Doubleday Dell Books for Young
Readers, a division of Bantam Doubleday Dell Publishing Group, Inc. "A Little
Rooster Book" and the portrayal of a rooster are trademarks of Bantam Doubleday
Dell Publishing Group, Inc. Bantam Doubleday Dell, 1540 Broadway, New York,
New York 10036.

PRINTED IN THE UNITED STATES OF AMERICA

UPR   0 9 8 7 6 5 4 3 2 1

Hi! Lamb Chop and I are going to tell you the story of *Cinderella*. Have you ever heard it? Lamb Chop loves this story because it has a happy ending, but sometimes she gets mixed up when we tell it—so you'll have to help her. Are you ready? Turn the page!

Once upon a time in a town far away lived a young girl named Cinderella.

Cinderella lived with her wicked stepmother and her two wicked stepsisters.

One day, a messenger from the royal castle knocked on their door with an invitation from the king. All the rich ladies of the land were invited to attend a fancy dress ball. And it was announced that at the ball the prince would pick . . .

No, no. The prince was going to pick someone to be his . . .

MAGICIAN

CLOWN

BRIDE

Cinderella helped her stepmother and stepsisters make beautiful gowns, but all she had to wear were rags, and she was not allowed to go to the fancy dress ball.

As her stepmother and stepsisters waved good-bye, Cinderella sat and cried because she was feeling so very . . .

. . . WET!

No, no. Cinderella was feeling very . . .

SAD   HAPPY   TIRED

Cinderella was very sad indeed. But suddenly, out of nowhere, there magically appeared Cinderella's fairy . . .

"Why are you crying, Cinderella?" her fairy godmother asked.
Cinderella wailed, "I'm the only one who isn't going to the fancy dress ball."
The fairy godmother told Cinderella to go into the vegetable garden and pick a really big, orange . . .

. . . CARROT!

No, no, Lamb Chop, not a carrot. She had to pick a really big . . .

After Cinderella picked the really big pumpkin, her fairy godmother told her to catch six mice. Then she raised her wand over the pumpkin and the mice, and turned the pumpkin into a splendid coach, pulled by six beautiful . . .

No, not monkeys. Six beautiful . . .

Now Cinderella had a splendid coach with six beautiful horses to take her to the ball. But she needed one more thing. So her fairy godmother touched Cinderella's head with her magic wand and gave her . . .

. . . A HEADACHE !

No. The fairy godmother gave her a beautiful gown to wear instead of her rags. And to her surprise, on her feet, Cinderella saw that she was wearing two glass . . .

No, no. Cinderella was wearing two glass . . .

The fairy godmother told Cinderella to listen for the clock to strike twelve bells, so that she would be home by midnight.

Well, when Cinderella got to the ball, the prince thought Cinderella was so nice, he danced only with her.

ISN'T THAT SWEET?

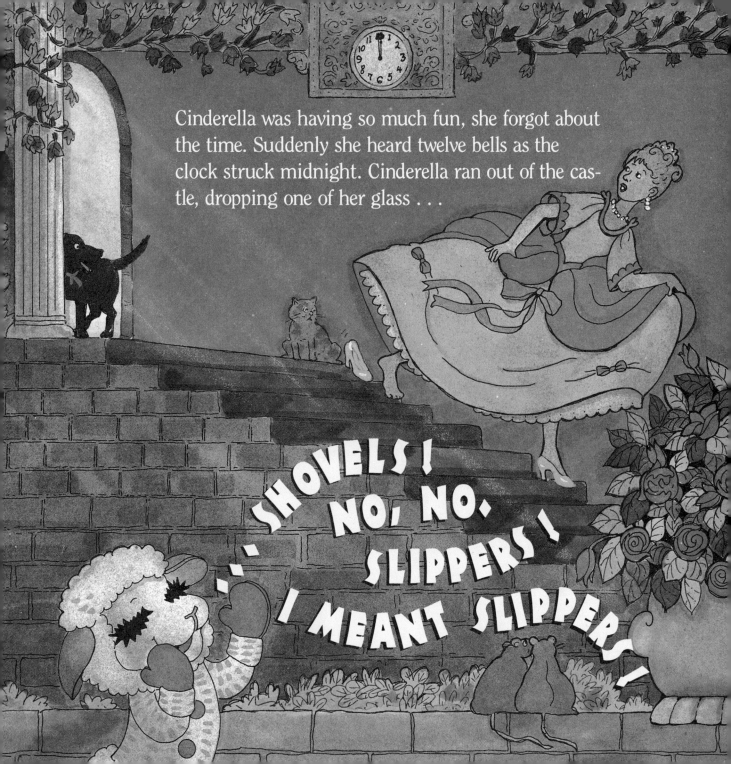

Cinderella was having so much fun, she forgot about the time. Suddenly she heard twelve bells as the clock struck midnight. Cinderella ran out of the castle, dropping one of her glass . . .

". . . SHOVELS! NO, NO, SLIPPERS! I MEANT SLIPPERS!"

Cinderella jumped into her coach and hurried home.
The prince ran after her but he couldn't catch her. He
picked up the glass slipper she had dropped and vowed
that he would marry the woman whose foot fit into it.

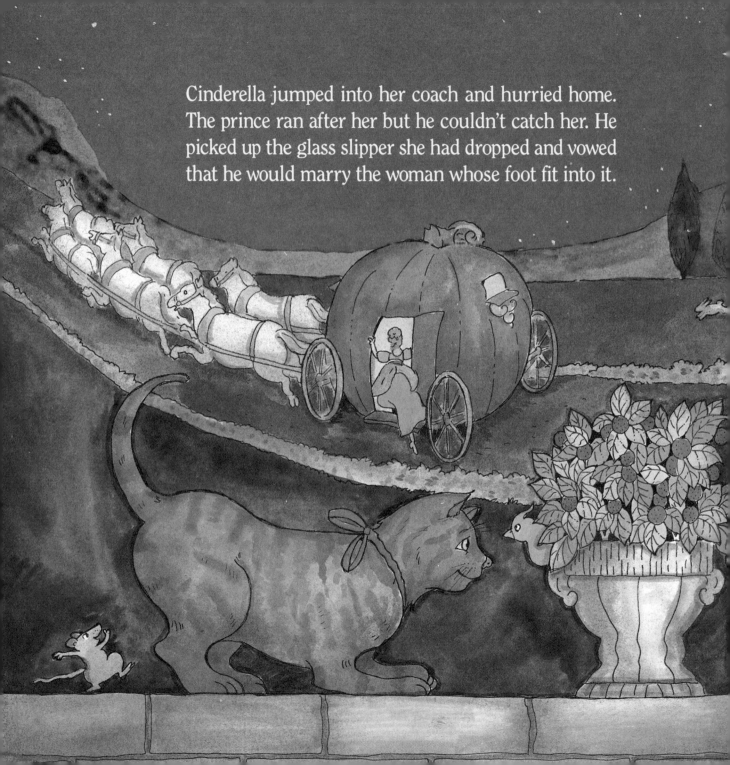

The next day, the prince went from house to house, asking every lady in the kingdom to try on the slipper. When he reached Cinderella's house, he tried the shoe on each of the two wicked . . .

. . . STEPLADDERS!

No, no, Lamb Chop. Now, for the last time—it's . . .

The stepsisters could not fit their big feet into the shoe.

No one fit into it until Cinderella tried on the glass . . .

. . . SLIPPER!

The slipper fit perfectly on Cinderella's foot, and she put on the other glass slipper as well. The prince and Cinderella invited everybody to come to the royal castle for their big wedding, and that's the happy ending to this story.